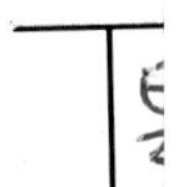

Snappy Dresser

'Snappy Dresser'
An original concept by Jenny Moore

Illustrated by Hannah McCaffery

Published by MAVERICK ARTS PUBLISHING LTD

Studio 11, City Business Centre, 6 Brighton Road,

Horsham, West Sussex, RH13 5BB

+44 (0)1403 256941

A CIP catalogue record for this book is available at the British Library.

ISBN 978-1-84886-835-9

Turquoise

This book is rated as: Turquoise Band (Guided Reading)

Snappy Dresser

by
Jenny Moore

illustrated by
Hannah McCaffery

Curtis the crocodile loved clothes. He wore the coolest jeans and the smartest shirts.

Curtis spent hours at the shops, buying new things to wear.

He spent hours in front of the mirror, trying on hats and ties. He was much too busy to play.

"Come on, Curtis," said his friends. "There's more to life than clothes. Why don't you come to the swamp with us?"

But Curtis didn't want to play in the swamp. "What about my jeans?" he said. "They'll get grubby. What about my shoes? I don't want to scuff them. What about my new hat? It might get wet."

Getting messy didn't sound like much fun to Curtis.

“Come on, Curtis,” begged his friends.

“We’re making a new mud slide today. It’s going to be the biggest, fastest slide ever!”

Curtis did like slides. But he didn't want to spoil his clothes.

“No thanks,” he said. “You’ll have to make it without me. I’m going shopping for a new jacket instead.”
“Alright,” said his friends. “You know where to find us if you change your mind.”

The other crocodiles headed down to the swamp, leaving Curtis all alone.
“I don’t need to make a mud slide,” he told himself and went into town.

There were so many different jackets to choose from.

Curtis tried on posh velvet jackets and stripy suit jackets. He tried on big puffy winter jackets and thin summer jackets.

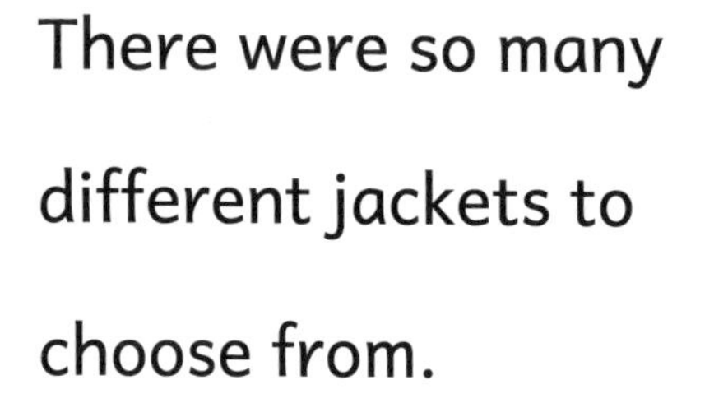

He tried on

jackets with zips

and jackets with buttons.

Curtis tried on so many jackets that

he lost count.

Shopping wasn't as much fun as usual though.

Curtis kept thinking about his friends at the swamp.

He kept thinking about the big slide they were making. He imagined zooming into the swamp with a big muddy splash.

That's when Curtis had his brilliant idea.

"Do you have any swamp jackets?" he asked the shop lady. "Or a muddy slide jacket?"

The lady shook her head. "What about a rain jacket?" she said.

"Alright," agreed Curtis. "I'll take it."

Next, Curtis went to the camping shop and bought a pair of blue waterproof trousers.

He bought red wellies at the shoe shop and a green rain hat at the hat shop.

Then he hurried home to try on his new clothes.

Curtis stared at himself in the mirror.

He loved his new look.

“Perfect for making a slide at the swamp,” he thought. “Perfect for playing with my friends. I hope I’m not too late.”

Curtis could hear laughter coming from the swamp. He could hear shouts and cheers and big splashing noises. He hurried through the trees to find his friends.

"Wait for me!" he called.

There it was! The biggest and best mud slide ever! Curtis raced over to join the other crocodiles.

"Wahhhh!" One of his new wellies slipped in the mud. Curtis fell over, landing in the mud with a big wet splat!

“Help!” called Curtis as the splat turned into a swoosh! He’d forgotten how slippery mud could be.

Curtis skidded right past the line of waiting crocodiles. He whooshed towards the slide at top speed.

Curtis shut his eyes as he reached the slide.

He was going too fast! He wasn't ready!

But it was too late to stop.

Curtis yelled as he zoomed down the slide.

But his yells soon turned to laughter.

"Woo-hoo!" he cried. "This is brilliant!"

His friends cheered as Curtis landed in the swamp with the biggest, muddiest splash ever!

Curtis had mud on his wellies and mud on his raincoat. He had mud on his trousers and he even had mud on his hat!

But the funny thing was, he didn't mind at all! Curtis's waterproof clothes were not spoiled, and he still looked cool!

Curtis grinned, heading straight back up the hill for another turn on the slide.

Curtis the crocodile still loved shopping for clothes.

But he always made sure he had time to play with his friends.

Quiz

1. Curtis the crocodile loved...

a) clothes

b) food

c) cleaning

2. What colour wellies did Curtis buy?

a) Blue

b) Green

c) Red

3. What kind of hat did Curtis buy?

a) A smart hat

b) A rain hat

c) A swimming hat

4. Why were Curtis's clothes not spoiled by the mud?

a) They were self-cleaning

b) They were waterproof

c) They were windproof

5. Curtis always made sure he had time to...

a) eat some food

b) play with his friends

c) clean his clothes

Turn over for answers

Pink

Red

Yellow

Blue

Green

Orange

Turquoise

Purple

Gold

White

Book Bands for Guided Reading

The Institute of Education book banding system is a scale of colours that reflects the various levels of reading difficulty. The bands are assigned by taking into account the content, the language style, the layout and phonics. Word, phrase and sentence level work is also taken into consideration.

Maverick Early Readers are a bright, attractive range of books covering the pink to white bands. All of these books have been book banded for guided reading to the industry standard and edited by a leading educational consultant.

To view the whole Maverick Readers scheme, visit our website at

www.maverickearlyreaders.com

Or scan the QR code above to view our scheme instantly!

Quiz Answers: 1a, 2c, 3b, 4b, 5b